Firebrand Firestorm

The Ancestors of Bjorn Esterday

Volume 08

Outrage

1704 & June 1776

Wynter Sommers

Published by Pure Force Enterprises, Inc.
California, USA
Since 2002

INGRAM
INGRAM® Distribution

ISBN-13: 978-1-7184-0020-7
ISBN-10: 1-7184-0020-9

DEDICATION

To those who are strong about truth,
justice, and the integrity of America;
your honorable actions make us proud.
To those who wonder if their daily
choices matter; your small decisions
impact generations to come.
To those everyday people who don't think
they have what it takes; when you strive
for extraordinary things, the impossible
becomes reality.
Your dreams today become our future
tomorrow.
Thank you for everything you do.

Bjorn Esterday
Was Not Born Yesterday
Series

Firebrand (15 Volumes+Conversation Station Book)
Edges (9 Stories +Conversation Station Book)
Gone (18 Stories + Conversation Station Book)

Bjorn EDGES Series

EDGES Book 1-Swift Encounter
EDGES Book 2-Rousing Attack
EDGES Book 3-One Foot Under
EDGES Book 4-Earthshake
EDGES Book 5-Broken String
EDGES Book 6-Key Witness
EDGES Book 7-Who is She?
EDGES Book 8-Vanish
EDGES Book 9-Chase or Die

Bjorn Series Alternate Reading Plan

1st	Edges Book 1		22nd	Gone Book 10
2nd	Edges Book 2		23rd	Firebrand Vol 9
3rd	Gone Book 1		24rd	Gone Book 11
4th	Firebrand Vol 1		25th	Firebrand Vol 10
5th	Edges Book 3		26th	Gone Book 12
6th	Firebrand Vol 2		27th	Gone Book 13
7th	Gone Book 2		28th	Firebrand Vol 11
8th	Gone Book 3		29th	Gone Book 14
9th	Firebrand Vol 3		30th	Firebrand Vol 12
10th	Gone Book 4		31st	Gone Book 15
11th	Firebrand Vol 4		32nd	Firebrand Vol 13
12th	Gone Book 5		33rd	Gone Book 16
13th	Gone Book 6		34th	Firebrand Vol 14
14th	Edges Book 4		35th	Gone Book 17
15th	Firebrand Vol 5		36th	Firebrand Vol15 (End)
16th	Gone Book 7		37th	Gone Book 18 (End)
17th	Firebrand Vol 6		38th	Edges Book 5
18th	Gone Book 8		39th	Edges Book 6
19th	Firebrand Vol 7		40th	Edges Book 7
20th	Gone Book 9		41st	Edges Book 8
21st	Firebrand Vol 8		42nd	Edges Book 9(End)

ACKNOWLEDGMENTS

We acknowledge those who actively build peace. We acknowledge all the selfless talent which contributed to creating meaningful tokens of consideration and sharing. We acknowledge that every person has a daily choice of right or wrong... and we thank you for choosing the right, good, honorable path filled with integrity because that is the difficult and brave path. Small choices today become lasting monuments of loving hope tomorrow.

CONTENTS

0 PREFACE

Eunice, TallMan's English born mother, was explaining how she, as a seven year old child, became captured to be a slave because her family did not believe in the monarch who paid the Indian tribe to attack her village. They were slave candidates because they dissented from those who wanted to be in power. Polly also, being Irish, fled the unformed colonies because she had been indentured, a paid form of slavery. Both women, unable to control their origin of birth, yearned for freedom and endured a traumatic struggle to discern the balance between slavery and patience until they could be free.

How did Eunice, a refined English girl who had just seen her mother slain for tripping while on a forced march along a 100 mile trail, who witnessed the death of her own baby sister and brother during the raid, react to an unexpected adoption by the fierce warrior tribe of Mohawks?

1 CHAPTER 70: (JUNE 1776) Polly Meets New Friends

Polly Mulhoolin enjoyed being a guest of Mr. and Mrs. Dunlap, owners of the print shop in town. They had an abundance of books to pass the time while she waited for her baby to arrive.

Just now, Polly was startled to hear Mrs. Dunlap abruptly announce she had been secretly trying to find out if Polly's husband, Button, was still alive. She had found no information, but she did meet a new friend, which Simms, the Dunlap butler, was bringing in at this very moment.

Polly was neither prepared to meet new friends, nor did she feel she was in a state to meet anybody as she was still great with child.

The only thing that calmed Polly's nerves was the thought that she would not be in this position had Jane Hargreaves been unable to stop and rescue her from certain death that one day as she stumbled out onto the road. Polly had met a friend and that friend and her servants saved Polly's life. So, it was not proper for Polly to become even a bit upset over a social faux pas. Since their first meeting, her hostess, Mrs. Dunlap, had always been so generous, and did truly wish to encourage Polly by introducing her to new friends. Polly determined to receive these strangers graciously and with gratitude to Mrs. Dunlap for fostering this new introduction.

Simms, the Dunlap butler, led two guests from the parlor into the library where Polly sat reading.

Mrs. Dunlap had yanked the cord again to alert Simms, her butler, to bring in the two guests awaiting in the parlor. She laughed to herself when her butler appeared in the door-frame with two strangers behind him.

"Oh! You startled me, Simms," Mrs. Dunlap laughed. "You are so good at being invisible sometimes."

Simms replied, "May I introduce your guests, Mrs. Dunlap? Or would you prefer to?"

The woman next to Simms looked about the age of Polly's own mother. The one Polly had left behind in Ireland. Next to the woman stood a tall, almost statuesque man. The woman had European features but was clothed in a doe-skin dress. Her hair was in two braids. The tall man had more Indian features, but he wore the shirt of a

European tradesman along with his leather britches.

Mrs. Dunlap responded to Simms, "I'll introduce them. Thank you, Simms. Please fetch the tea." The Dunlap butler, Simms, left silently.

Mrs. Dunlap addressed all the guests, "As you know, these attacks, such as the one on Polly's home, have become quite frequent. We do not have any central location where one can report they are missing another human being and expect any assistance on finding them. Alas, in lieu of finding any information on your husband, Polly, I have brought you two new delightful souls to befriend."

Polly looked down at the carpet, a bit disappointed, but aware that Mrs. Dunlap was trying to make the best of an awkward situation.

Polly took a deep breath, then looked up and smiled at the woman and then the man.

Mrs. Dunlap stood to the side of the woman and man and announced to Polly, "Polly, I'd like you to meet Uh... Eunice or Marguerite..." Mrs. Dunlap whispered to Polly, "that's her Catholic name..." Then Mrs. Dunlap resumed her speaking voice and continued to announce, "...and her son, who is taking her home to Canada. They delayed their travel plans to have a spot of tea with us. Isn't that grand?"

Mrs. Dunlap showed the man and woman where they could sit.

Mrs. Dunlap continued to explain to a speechless Polly, "They insist having us call them by their first Christian names, as if we are their family, before having even befriended them. Isn't that so casual and modern?"

Polly stuttered, "Oh. Um. Hello. It is a pleasure to make your acquaintance."

Mrs. Dunlap continued speaking to Polly, "...I prefer the name Eunice. More British-like, you see. Marguerite just seems too... well... French." Mrs. Dunlap laughed, "But she will respond should you call her by either name."

Mrs. Dunlap nodded at the woman, who politely nodded in reply.

Simms returned with a tray of tea. Servants set out the tea for each of the four and then quietly left the room under the silent direction of Simms, the butler.

Mrs. Dunlap turned to the woman she had just introduced as Eunice and motioned toward Polly with a gesture, then said to Eunice, "She's very casual, as well. You can call her Polly. She's Irish, you see... but, like you... the Irish do things differently." Mrs. Dunlap smiled at Polly then added, "I've already told them your story, Polly."

"My story?" Polly repeated, somewhat confused.

"Yes. All of it." Mrs. Dunlap smiled, "Well, it wasn't as if it was a secret, was it?" Mrs. Dunlap popped a biscuit into her mouth, then remarked, "Oh, Cook really did a marvelous job on these. Just perfect." She turned to Eunice, the woman and said, "Try one. My chef, her name is Mrs. Cook, made these. You'll love them. "

Mrs. Dunlap offered the plate to Eunice, who silently took one, bit it and smiled.

Then, Mrs. Dunlap offered the plate to the son of Eunice, "And I must apologize, as I have forgotten your name."

He responded with, "TallMan."

The statuesque man smiled at his mother, Eunice, before extending a polite hand to Polly. Eunice clarified, "I gave my son a Christian name, but he insists on using his tribal name."

"I see you are from an Indian tribe," Polly said while looking at Mrs. Dunlap as if she had betrayed Polly's sacred trust.

Then Eunice replied, "I've brought you a gift, Polly. A book I thought you would like."

Polly was taken aback. Not only was Eunice's English perfect, but a complete stranger had brought her a gift? Polly didn't quite know what to think or if she should have reciprocated.

Eunice continued, "After Mrs. Dunlap shared your story with us, I thought the way my son and I dress might cause you some consternation." She smiled, again, and handed the book to Polly. Eunice then leaned back and settled against the soft pillows on Mrs. Dunlap's chair.

Polly accepted the book, but struggled to find the right words for this situation. She attempted a couple of times, but managed only to utter syllables and not full words. Polly closed her mouth and looked down at the book in her lap.

Eunice said, "I was not always part of an Indian tribe. I was born Eunice Williams, a very British name, indeed.

Later, I became *Marguerite Kanenstenhawi Arosen, of the Bear tribe,* married to a man from the Wolf tribe. My son, TallMan, has been on a quest to find the best medicines of many lands. He has completed his journeys and we are on our way back to Canada, where my home is."

"I... I... I," Polly started haltingly, "I have heard nothing of you nor your son. I thank you for the gift, but I must apologize for not knowing what to say."

Mrs. Dunlap tossed a limp hand at Polly, "Nonsense, Polly. I brought them here so you could listen to them. You don't need to worry about being entertaining, just attentive."

Polly was about to interject a comment, but Mrs. Dunlap continued, "I knew if I had asked you to receive them in advance, you would have said no. That is why I," Mrs. Dunlap searched for the words, "ambushed you."

Mrs. Dunlap giggled to herself, took a sip of hot tea, then replaced her china cup in the saucer, and continued, "I could never tell Eunice's story the way she could. You have to hear it directly from her."

"TallMan," Eunice started, "has met both scoundrels and friends during his travels. He has learned from other tribes, as well as from the Dutch, the French, Spanish and English. I have daughters waiting for me back home, but my son has become an unlikely ambassador of justice."

"TallMan... that is an unusual name..." Polly said to herself, not realizing others heard her say it as well.

"How is it different from the English Longfellow as a family name? It contains a descriptive word and a noun, just as mine does..." TallMan smiled.

Polly blushed embarrassed, "I see. So... You are a man of medicine?"

"Yes. I feel I must," TallMan said softly to Polly in an attempt to put her at ease, "...heal when I can. Be that the wound is on a body, or be the wound of an injustice done to a group of people. I hope to let the innocent remain free of false accusations as much as I wish a body to be free of ailments."

"Um. I see...." Polly said unable say anything else.

"One must make sense during these senseless times," Mrs. Dunlap concurred.

"Flowers?" Polly asked, looking down at the book in her lap. "You gave me a book about flowers?"

"Oh, that is more than a book," Eunice went on to explain, "...It is a lesson to remember. The information in that volume was collated and illustrated by Jane Colden from New York. Originally from Scotland. "

"I have not heard of her," Polly explained.

13

"When she was a teenager," Eunice went on, "Jane Colden corresponded with botanists and naturalists, including Linnaeus. She even mastered the Linnaean classification system and collected 300 regional plants and cataloged them with her sketches."

"So interesting," Mrs. Dunlap commented toward Polly, then urged Eunice to continue, "Do, go on..."

Eunice continued, "Jane Colden discovered a flower and produced a New York Flora catalog. She inquired about her floral discovery in 1759, but the Edinburgh Philosophical Society never replied. She married Farquhar, a doctor, and had a son... Then she sadly died at age 42. Four years later, the Philosophical society published Jane Colden's newly discovered gardenia genus in their journal, but because she was already dead, a Scottish botanist, Alexander Garden was given credit for her discovery, hence the name 'gardenia. But the society says they admired Jane's accurate work and will keep all her original essays on file for other naturalists to reference."

"That is quite fascinating indeed, but why tell me the story, of a Jane Colden, who never got credit for her own botanical discovery..." Polly smiled as politely as possible.

"Because, Polly," Eunice started, "when Mrs. Dunlap found me, quite by chance, and explained your situation to me, I felt compelled to encourage you. Don't be like Jane Colden and just ignore your talents. You can be married, have children, and still use the skills which God has given you. Do not give up the search for your husband. Do not assume he is dead, yet. Do not underestimate the impact you can have on this still forming and very new world."

"I confess," Polly replied, "I have also donned the comfortable moccasins and such when we built our cabin, which is probably cinders and ash by now. We once had a dream to build 30 cabins on hundreds of acres of my very own land, but..." Polly lamented.

"Perhaps you can adjust your dream," Eunice encouraged, "to build 29 instead of 30 cabins."

"How can one hold onto such a lofty dream, when one will surely just be attacked, again?" Polly asked.

TallMan replied, "I am Indian. My mother is English born. Her Indian family is of the Bear clan. My father is of the Wolf clan. My mother's tribe converted to Catholicism... so if you were me, which group would you consider yours? Am I not a blend of all of them?"

Polly responded with, "I don't understand your point, Mr. TallMan."

"My point is," TallMan explained, "that among any people, greed can make a man turn against his own kind. Each man has a choice: resist or succumb. Likewise, you must make your own deliberate choices, Polly."

Mrs. Dunlap interjected, "Polly doesn't have any issues with greed, TallMan. I think she is quite aware that evil could lurk in the hearts of men who may compromise morality for the allure of power or money. But, I brought you here to share a story."

Mrs. Dunlap refilled TallMan's cup with steaming hot water and poured in a dash of milk, which seemed to confuse TallMan, who was used to more basic unadorned foods.

Mrs. Dunlap turned to Eunice, "Please tell Polly just the way you told me earlier." Mrs. Dunlap offered Eunice a platter of tea treats to nibble.

2 CHAPTER 71: (1704) Eunice's Story

In the Dunlap living room sat Polly, Mrs. Dunlap, the Indian medicine man TallMan and his mother, the English Born Eunice.

Eunice took a bite of her biscuit and then a sip of hot tea. "Where shall I begin?" Eunice asked.

Polly inquired, "When you came from England, where did you first settle?"

"Ah," Eunice smiled, "Back in 1704, I was but a seven year old girl when our village was raided by French, Abenaki, and Mohawk Indians. I was then taken to Canada with about one hundred other captives. Queen Anne's battles resulted in the death of Indians, Spanish, Colonists, and British. This raid meant the death of my six week old sister, Jerusha and my brother John Williams Jr. On the journey north, my mother tripped and fell. So, she was also killed. My father had escaped. At the early age of seven, I knew I had to keep up with my captors in order to stay alive."

"That is horrific! You must feel such resentment toward those who had imprisoned your family," Polly blurted out.

"No... Not anymore. I had to realize that the men who herded us were paid to. They did not feel they were doing wrong. I clung to my childlike Christian faith and realized hating those men did nothing good. I had to say goodbye to my kin and make the best out of an unknown future before me."

Polly closed her eyes and murmured, "I must say... I still awaken in the middle of the night with such horrid vivid memories of hearing the attack on our cabin, I do not know if I could forgive, as you did your captors...Were you taken to be sold as a slave, then?"

3 CHAPTER 72: (1705) Catholic Mohawks

Continuing her story, Eunice nestled into the soft pillows of the Dunlap sofa. Mrs. Dunlap, TallMan, and Polly were all quietly attentive as Eunice continued her story.

"One year later, in 1705," Eunice started.

"Girl. Girl," one of the Indians had pushed small eight-year-old Eunice Williams into a crowd of other children. These shepherds of the prisoners had only limited English but Eunice, now nearly a year with the tribe located in Quebec Canada, had learned a smattering of their words.

What little Eunice did not know was that she was going to travel to her new home, even further from the colonies where she had originally been captured.

After a long and exhausting walk, which lasted days, little Eunice arrived.

She wondered at the sight of a crucifix hanging on the wall. Were all savages Catholics? Did Catholics come to try and convert these people?

Eunice was raised to recognize an empty cross, which symbolized the resurrection of Christ. Jesus, God's son, died on a cross as the ultimate sacrifice, Eunice recalled from her Puritan teachings. He died so when people sinned, they could be forgiven instead of sacrificing themselves. It was the death to stop all other sacrifices. Jesus had risen from the dead, as she recalled when celebrating Easter, and that is why the cross was empty. It was a reminder that Jesus was in Heaven, still alive.

But, Eunice did recall the version where a carved image of Jesus was still hanging on the cross, in the midst of dying. Dying for her sins. What sins could an eight year old commit, she wondered.

Then, she remembered her failings back in the Colony. Her stubborn attitude. Her complaining. She recalled her father telling her that Catholics used their image of the dying Jesus on the cross because they wanted to remember the suffering Jesus endured on the cross. Whereas the Puritans looked at the completed cycle of resurrection. Yes. Jesus died as the final sacrifice for our sins, but he was raised into Heaven and returned.

She recalled the story her father read to her in the Bible where over five hundred people saw the resurrected Jesus walking among them before he went back to Heaven. It was somewhere in First Corinthians, chapter fifteen. The Catholics looked at the pain of the sacrifice, to remind them that God allowed his son to die in their place. It was intended, Eunice reasoned, to stop them from sinning in the first place.

Puritans looked at the blessing and joy of the completed sacrifice, choosing to remember that sometimes one must pass through difficult times, but if one acts with loving integrity then the peace of God will rest upon your soul.

Same act of sacrifice. Different perspective. Catholics or Puritans.

They both believed Jesus was the son of God and that Jesus died and rose again three days later. Was that the only difference between those Indians who lived in the wild and the colonists who lived in houses?

Little eight year old Eunice looked around.

She saw the tribes-people going about their daily activities. She noticed only a few spoke English and not very well. She would need to learn their language. That would be her sacrifice. She would try to communicate with them and not focus on the trauma which had brought her to this place in this moment. She would see Jesus as her example.

Eunice broke away from the cluster of people who had been collected from raids, brought to Quebec, rounded up again a year later when these Indians had captured enough slaves, and marched the grieving unfortunates to this place. She wondered if they would monitor her closely, as they did in Quebec.

Across the way, she saw a boy from her group. Older than she was. He spoke French. A man from the tribe approached this French boy and seemed to communicate with him. They both conversed for a few moments. Alas,

Eunice did not have a command of French. She only knew English, yet there did not seem to be another English speaker around.

The boy walked back to the larger group of colonists and simply stood there. Exhausted.

One of the Indian men, from the Quebec camp who had led the Colonists on a very long journey to this place, started to walk into the center of the colonist crowd. Eunice thought of him as the Head Walker, since he was always in front and motioned when to stop and rest and when to continue walking.

The Head Walker split the group in half by walking between the crowd and taking one, pushing him to one side, and then taking another and pushing that one to the other side. He would bark at them if they moved from their spot. These tattered and exhausted colonists obeyed, having witnessed this man viciously use the Tomahawk with great accuracy.

The older French boy was now pushed to one side to join another, smaller group. Eunice was in neither group. She was standing on the outskirts and observed this group-splitting activity as if she were in the audience watching, not participating.

Cautiously, after a moment, little Eunice approached the man who had just spoken to the French boy. She would call him a Language Fellow. Perhaps this Language Fellow knew other European Languages. Perhaps this man could explain what was happening and why she was not being put in either group.

Eunice watched.

Then, Eunice turned to the Language Fellow, who spoke European languages, and asked slowly, "Where they go?"

The man of languages replied, "You stay, Girl. This home."

Eunice turned to look at the others.

The two smaller groups of colonists were assigned their own Indian Head Walker. Two. One for each group. Other Indians brought up the rear of both groups.

The weary colonists were all handed a morsel of food, which they hungrily consumed while still standing. After a few moments, the Indians in the rear pushed the group toward the Head Walker. As if responding to a signal, each Head Walker took his group in a direction opposite from the other.

Little Eunice was ignored, still not part of either group. Both groups were now leaving this place and leaving Eunice behind.

A bit more urgently, Eunice returned to the Language Fellow and asked, "Where they go? Do I go with them?"

"No. You stay, Girl. This home," Language Fellow replied.

She now saw the backs of both groups heading off in opposite directions. So.

This place is her new home. This place. Where and what was this place?

Eunice turned to Language Fellow, again, and asked, "Where is home?" The man smiled, pleased Eunice now understood, "Kahnawake. "

He said it again, rather slowly and smiled when Eunice repeated it. "Kah...Kaaaah...naaaaa...wakeeeee..." Eunice repeated.

The man smiled. "Home," he said and he pointed to a crucifix and held out some pages of a Bible.

These pages were not bound in a book. It was as if somebody had ripped them out of a Bible and given them to Language Fellow.

Perhaps this Language Fellow was the official tribe appointed keeper of the Holy Pages.

Little Eunice couldn't be sure, but when Language Fellow handed her a single page, she took it and examined the words. It looked as if the pages were printed in French. Language Fellow had extracted the pages from a tanned leather strip, cut to be larger than the Bible pages. Leather strings were attached to this larger leather sheet to allow the pages to be placed in the middle, then rolled up and protected by this outer leather, as if it were a book cover, which protected Holy Words on the aged sheets. Obviously, Language Fellow had great respect for these scraps of scripture.

Eunice shook her head trying to convey that she could not read the French Bible pages and quietly handed the pages back to Language Fellow. He accepted them with a smile and gently positioned the holy pages in the center of the leather cover and rolled them up, tying the string to protect the pages.

Little Eunice knew how to read some English, but her father had not yet taught her much French.

Eunice said, "It looks like the book of Psalms." She paused. "Psalms," Eunice reiterated as she pointed to the big word on at the top of the page.

The man smiled, repeating, "Psalms." Then he pointed to another word and said, "Jesuit man."

Eunice assumed Language Fellow was trying to communicate that a French Jesuit missionary must have influenced this tribe a while ago, leaving Language Fellow in charge of the fragments of the Bible.

Eunice sighed and smiled thinking she would have preferred that an English speaking missionary had done the converting.

She smiled again, curtsied, and left Language Fellow.

Back home, in the Colonies, Little Eunice Williams was considered a weak and sickly girl. When she felt physically weak, she also felt mentally weak and was not as swift as others her age with book studies.

Her parents were thankful she had survived the grueling voyage from Europe to the colonies in the first place. Her father felt it best to give her a simple diet of boiled gruel each day. He was concerned her body would be unable to digest any of the varieties offered in the Colonies.

Luckily, she recalled her father telling her mother that daughters only needed to learn how to be good wives and she was too young for that, so best to let her rest in hopes she would grow up to find a man to marry and provide for her.

Women needed men to guide them.

As Eunice recalled the thought, she looked around. There were no men here to help her.

She was the only Colonist now left behind with this tribe.

All the other colonists who knew her ways had just left. She could still see them in the distance, walking farther and farther away.

She was, indeed, the only one of her kind, here, the only one who really spoke English. She had nowhere to run to... She began to realize that this was indeed her new home, her new "family".

Eunice heard the sound of children laughing. She looked around to ascertain from where the sound originated. She found a group of children playing. They were running around. She never ran and played. It was difficult for girls in corsets to run about. Yet, these children seemed to be... enjoying this activity.

Still curious, Eunice walked away from the playing children and into what looked to be a chapel. This plan was designed with branches, stones and layers of bark. It looked as if the builders tried to make it long lasting.

She glanced around. There was

another rough building, much larger... and longer over there. Eunice presumed it was the Jesuits who may have built this chapel. Those who lived in the tribe must have put up the other, longer structure... the far one, way over there.

Above the front entrance was a wooden cross, a make-shift crucifix. Eunice quietly walked through the door.

Inside the chapel was a wooden tablet in a prominent position upon the alter. The numbers 1676 were carved on it.

"Ah," Eunice thought to herself, "So this building must be about thirty years old."

She pieced the bits of the puzzle together. Here she was, the sole English-speaking person. In a land named "Kahnawake".

Age eight.

This tribe of Indians must have been converted to Catholicism by a French

Jesuit missionary sometime around the year 1676.

Just then, a woman of the tribe entered the chapel and got down on her knees to be the same height as Little Eunice. The woman said something to the child, which Eunice could not understand.

The woman pointed to her, then took Eunice by the hand and walked outside to point to the others and said, "Mohawk."

"Moooowhaaawk," Eunice repeated. The woman smiled.

Eunice wondered if that was the name of this tribe and the K-word she learned earlier was the name of the land... or the other way around. Eunice remembered the word and squeezed the hand of the woman to get her attention.

When the woman looked down at little Eunice, Eunice said, "Kahnawake".

The woman smiled as a tear welled up in her eyes.

She kneeled on the ground to be eye level with little Eunice and hugged her.

Eunice was confused. Who was this woman and why was she so... friendly?

Then, the woman felt the rib area of Eunice and became perplexed. Eunice concluded the woman did not understand that Eunice was wearing a corset. Eunice concluded none of the tribes had any undergarment even resembling a corset. It was the proper attire for a lady in the colonies. The woman briskly took Eunice by the hand and walked into the other structure Eunice had spied earlier... the long building.

Inside, it was similar to a hallway, but with no rooms on either side, just areas set apart for one purpose or another. This was not like anything Eunice had seen before.

Eunice ran her hand along the side of the wall and she recalled the distinctive smell of elm. She looked at the wall. It was covered with sheets of bark from an elm tree. But this hall appeared to be nearly a hundred feet long.

The sides of the inside of this building seemed to be propped up by smooth sticks. The sticks which ran from the top of one wall to the next had food drying over them. Above, in the roof... or maybe it was the ceiling... holes were cut out and Eunice concluded it must be their brick-free version of a chimney.

Indeed, when Eunice looked at the ground directly below these holes, she saw a carefully set up fire. This was their hearth. Looking around at the food, she saw dried meats, vegetables and even something which could have been baked. There was no gruel in sight. How very odd, Eunice thought.

While Eunice was preoccupied taking in all this new information and wondering whether these tribes people ate, slept or did something else in this room, she became aware that the woman who had brought her in here was speaking to her, as if Eunice was expected to understand.

The woman was holding up a soft doe skin dress. A dress? It looked about the right size for a girl like Eunice.

The woman then knelt down and smiling with a tear in her eye, said in very broken English, "Strong like Bear family." She handed the dress to Eunice. It looked much more comfortable than what Eunice herself was wearing, constricted as she was by her own corset and long gown.

The woman helped her change from her own dress into this doe-skin garment. The woman then brought Eunice to the entrance and pointed to the same group of children playing, which Eunice had seen earlier.

Once more, the woman spoke in halting English and touched Eunice's hand, saying, "Daughter." Then she touched herself and said, "Mother." After that, the woman gently pushed Eunice outside in the direction of the children.

Uncertain how to join whatever game these children were playing, Eunice stopped at the edge of the grassy area where the children ran about.

She watched silently, and from time to time looked down at this new doe skin dress she was now wearing. It seemed just like the ones the Indian girls had on.

One of the Indian children saw her, a girl of about Eunice's age. She ran up to Eunice and said something, but Eunice didn't understand. The girl just looked up over Eunice's shoulder at the woman who had given Eunice the dress. Eunice turned around. That woman was still standing behind Eunice a few yards away.

The woman shouted something to the Indian girl standing in front of Eunice. Eunice would name her Cheerful. The

Cheerful girl got a huge grin on her face and took Eunice by the hand, bringing her into the circle of playing children.

As Eunice stumbled behind this very direct and cheerful girl, Eunice twisted around to look back at the woman. She was still watching Eunice and had brought both her hands up to her mouth. It looked as if she were praying and seemed a little worried.

Eunice wondered if that woman really would be her new mother and this, her new home... but for how long?

4 CHAPTER 73: (JUNE 1776) Reaction to Eunice Adoption

Polly sat up, holding her hand palm up to stop Eunice from continuing her story. She looked at Mrs. Dunlap, who, Polly assumed, had heard Eunice's story earlier. Polly noticed Mrs. Dunlap seemed enthralled to hear it all again.

A servant entered the room to replace the tea water with a fresh pot, and silently vanished again from the room.

Polly asked Eunice, "So a year after you were taken by Indians, in 1705, you

41

joined a settlement of Catholic Mohawks?"

"Kahnawake," Eunice clarified, "to become adopted by the Bear clan."

"I dare say, that does not sound as if you were going to be auctioned or sold as a slave, at all!" Polly declared.

Eunice continued, "The woman who introduced herself as 'mother', gave me the name of *A'ongonte* or *Wa'ongote.*"

"What does that mean in English, dear?" Mrs. Dunlap asked.

Eunice explained, "It can be translated to mean a 'person who has been replanted' or 'one who is planted like an Ash tree'".

"Very poetic name, that is..." Polly remarked, "Did you form a relationship with your new Indian mother?"

Eunice answered, "Later on, I discovered that my Indian mother, as you call her, had lost her own daughter to smallpox, a disease brought here by the European colonists like my original family. She did not blame me as a carrier of a plague, which killed her daughter, her only child. Rather, this mother saw me as an answer to her prayers. I lost a mother. She lost a daughter... we accepted each other. I saw her as 'mother', not 'Indian mother'. When I was older, I officially became a Catholic and was given the name Marguerite around 1710, five years later."

"So, by that time, you spent seven years in the Colony and now six years in the tribe. Did you ever see your father, again?" Polly asked.

Eunice looked at her son, TallMan, then at Polly and leaned forward.

"I did," Eunice started. This was a tender subject for Eunice, who looked up at the ceiling and seemed to blink away tears recalling a moment in her past which still evoked emotion.

Eunice continued, "It took him years to negotiate a ransom for me, but by then I had forgotten my English. My father could not speak to me, nor I to him. He loved me and I loved the memory I had of him, but I had forgotten English and European mannerisms."

Mrs. Dunlap gasped in horror, "How did you manage without European manners?"

Eunice explained, "I could not call any of the colonies home. The family, which adopted me, loved me. My father saw that. He met my adopted parents and they were kind to him. A young translator explained how I was an answer to their prayers by giving them a daughter they had lost to a disease. My father softened when he understood. My father saw how strong and healthy I had become. Through a translator, he advised me to recite the Puritan catechism and pray for wisdom and said he would always love me."

Polly briefly recalled when she had

waved farewell to her own mother in Ireland, and said, "That must have been difficult to have said good bye to your father... even though he knew you were in a safe place."

"Yes..." Eunice sighed, "He said he would pray God would use me to heal this young country wounded by raids, greed, and human sins. I never saw myself playing so grand a scheme in life. I am content with my life as it is."

"You remained with the tribe?" Polly asked.

"I did," Eunice replied.

"Difficult to grasp," Mrs. Dunlap started, "That you had forgotten your English and needed a translator to speak to your own father. Your English now is nearly perfect."

Eunice looked at TallMan, her son, then back at Mrs. Dunlap and said, "Around 1713, I married a French Mohawk, Francois Xavier Arosen from the Wolf clan. He was the translator with my father. I then assumed the adult name of Kanenstenhawi, which means "She who brings in corn".

Mrs. Dunlap interrupted, "So, you went from 'one who was replanted' to 'one who brings in corn'?"

Eunice smiled, "For me to have the name of one who provides for the tribe was an honor. It meant I was responsible enough to have others rely on me for food. This was not a job I could have ever done if I had returned to the colonies. As a girl in the colonies, I was weak. As an adult in the tribe, I was skilled and valued. Do you know that realizing you are valued and appreciated makes you work with purpose to fulfill expectations of the tribe? "

"You learned skills? What sort of skills?" Polly asked.

Eunice explained, "I learned to plant, cultivate, harvest, and hunt. In a Puritan colony, those are tasks performed only men. Even then, some men would be viewed as too peaceful to engage in activities such as hunting. As a British colonial village woman, I could never lead a hunting party and... I... I... I was actually quite good at it. After I married, I had to re-learn English. This was a very slow process. I was determined to raise my own children with both my tongue of English and the language of the tribe, as well."

TallMan spoke, "I hated it when my mother would force me to learn English as a child. I felt it was useless and none of the others had to learn it, yet as an adult, I find my command of English intrigues the Europeans I encounter."

Eunice agreed, "I always enjoy the expression of a new acquaintance, who has already formed one opinion of you before you speak, and then quite another afterwards." Eunice smiled to herself as she recalled moments when she surprised others with her command of both languages.

Mrs. Dunlap asked, "How did the values of the tribe conflict with your Puritan values?"

Eunice looked gently at Polly and Mrs. Dunlap. Then Eunice continued with, "They did not conflict. Nowhere in the Bible does it say a woman must be constrained with a corset and stifle her God-given talents. No, the tribal leaders appreciated my contributions and I was using the gifts God gave me, as my father wanted."

"Is he still living?" Polly asked cautiously.

Eunice looked down at her tea cup on the table and said, "No. He died around 1729 when I was 32... and it made me sad to realize that now only a couple of my original Puritan siblings still lived in the colonies."

"Didn't you ever want to return home?" Polly asked.

Eunice replied, "My home is in Canada. Not the British American Colonies."

TallMan spoke, "When I was old enough to travel, I was curious about the land from which my mother came. Curious about the colonies..."

"What was your first impression, TallMan, when you first encountered us? The way we dress?" Mrs. Dunlap asked.

"I will be honest..." TallMan explained, "Among the British, I found that some men think they become powerful by hiding information."

TallMan gingerly continued, "Some husbands were judged by how much they were able to restrict the movements of his wife, keeping her in the home."

TallMan clearly explained, "I did not understand how a society could survive by stifling half of their population in such a manner. To me, this would simply breed a spirit of secret hatred...resentment... in women for having their talents suppressed. It would create a situation where a woman could not remove the frustration, causing her to act in deceitful... even manipulative... duplicitous ways."

"You have observed more than medicinal formulas on your travels, it seems," Mrs. Dunlap suggested.

Eunice continued as she took a sip of tea, "I visited my British siblings after my forty-second birthday, which was about a decade after father died. Ironically, I thought about the man I first met, the one I called Language Fellow. He had also died many years earlier. By then, I was married to the man who translated the message that my father still loved me very much. I was blessed to have a fine husband who was so good with languages and patient to teach me and our children. We all became familiar with French, Mohawk dialects, and English, which was my weakest, but I managed to still communicate while I was learning."

"After adopting the ways of the tribe,

did you feel comfortable when you visited your siblings in the Colonies?" Polly asked.

Eunice took a deep breath and looked at her hands, "I saw the contrasts in our cultures. We looked alike, but we did not share the same values, just the same parents. TallMan came to his own conclusions after seeing my siblings and their families and friends."

"After you returned to your tribe, did you keep in touch with your siblings?" Polly asked, feeling a bit homesick herself and now missing her own husband Button very much.

"My brother Stephen persisted in communicating with me. He lived in Massachusetts." Eunice leaned back and thought, "I visited in '41, '43, and '61, when I was 64 years old. A few years later, my husband died in 1765, leaving me a widow."

Mrs. Dunlap asked, "And when did your son, TallMan, think of exploring our humble lands to learn medicine?"

Eunice replied, "After I grieved over the loss of my husband for some time, our village was struck by a cruel ailment the LongCoats must have brought."

"LongCoats?" Polly asked.

"Oh... the white man," TallMan clarified. "I mean to say those of other countries who came to this land wearing such impractical long coats."

Eunice continued, "One victim of this disease was a woman my son loved deeply and wanted to marry. She died..." Eunice laid her hand on top of her son's in comfort, again, as she continued. "My husband died. My son's beloved died. So, TallMan was driven to explore... to learn more than our medicine men did. He did not want another to feel the heart-pain of a death which could have been avoided if treated properly..."

"And now," TallMan interjected as his voice cracked, "I have learned much. I am ready to come home... To take you home, Mother..."

"Indeed..." Mrs. Dunlap stated loudly in an overly cheerful tone to erase the somber cloud which had settled on the group, "Eunice, dear, when shall both you and your son commence the long carriage journey to Canada?"

5 CHAPTER 74: (JUNE 1776) The Barn Is Still Talking

Inside the barn, located just on the outskirts of Meeting Town, the conversation noise level started rising anew.

Livingston tried to respond to the challenging statement made earlier, which had cast doubts on his ability to pen a formal letter to the King of England. Frustrated, as the arguments around him drowned out his attempts to speak.

He waived his arms above the crowd, but nobody looked in his direction as they were all engaged in loud, competitive discussions.

Robert Livingston was determined to be heard. This group only had use of this barn until stable boys returned with the horses.

Finally, Livingston pushed a wooden crate near the wall where the reins hung. He grabbed a bridal and smacked the metal bit against the empty metal trough of water to create a loud clang. He then shouted to get the attention of the turbulent crowd.

As the attendees turned toward the noise, Livingston shouted his reply, "Indeed. Why not I? Have I not the best penmanship of all of you? It matters not if I believe unification can last more than a year or so. What matters is that we all cooperate and work toward a goal: The goal of unifying all your voices into a single powerful letter which the King shall not ignore."

Button now used the wall mounted horse reins as a ladder to gain height above the crowd.

And quite contrary to his nature, Button also shouted, "I am with this fellow! I had intended to remain silent, but have been compelled to speak out. We do need every town, every city, every county to vote and select a representative in our legislature."

Before Button could finish, ardent companions of Henry Mossop, the opera singer, shoved their way through the crowd to reach Button, shouting in an attempt to drown out the message Button was urgently trying to speak.

Button, however, clutched at the leather reins, using them as whips to smack away the clamoring hands trying to pull him down from the same wooden crate Mr. Livingston had occupied.

Button shouted, "We must break off business connections which stop us from being independent. Cease activity with any foe to the rights of freedom for our British American liberty. Ensure all goods shipped to our shores are inspected, and determined to be the finest quality, before we permit that ship to unload. If unified, we can set the standard of which goods we would accept and what level of quality we expect."

"Oh, and are we to set up a committee just to inspect incoming goods to ensure it meets to some standard?" One man in the audience sneered sarcastically, adding, "We cannot enforce such a practice! We must accept what the King sends us... no matter how poor the quality, nor how high the price."

Button turned toward that man, and roared, "If the price is too high, the residents of the colonies will not be able to afford it! It is reasonable to require all manufacturers located in our British America to sell their products to the citizens of British America at reasonable prices. We must discourage overly inflated prices. The colonists which make the product here in this land should also be the customer and be able to buy the same product."

The heckler retorted, scoffing at Button, "Ridiculous, Sir! You are proposing manufacturers in our colonies should price goods so the workers in their factories can afford to buy the very goods they make. How will we maintain our class structure if we allow that? Absurd!"

Exploding abruptly, Benjamin Franklin boomed at the entire assembly, shocking them into silence. "Enough! We shall not make progress if all you do is thunder your petty opinions. We have more at stake here, than your pride. Everyone! I demand Silence! Immediately!"

Robert Livingston stepped forward and lowered his voice. His throat was sore from the shouting he did earlier.

Livingston took a step forward, "Mr. Franklin. If we were to follow this man's suggestion," Livingston pointed to Button then turned back, "If we were to demand that manufacturers set affordable prices and enforce that demand, then we would eliminate the artificial shortage of goods our customers currently experience today."

Mr. Adams cleared his throat and added with hand on his hip, "And how are we, Mr. Livingston, expected to enforce our currently fragile concept of unity?" Mr. Adams asked as he looked around. "I challenge anyone to answer."

Button popped in with, "If we discuss options, we could formalize a unified, orderly and enforceable approach, I'm sure of it."

Henry Mossop, the frustrated opera singer, suddenly disgusted, guided a handful of his cohorts toward the exit.

"It will never work," the fading opera *primo uomo* boomed as he reached the large double door of the barn.

The same man, who seemed to simply enjoy being contrary to whomever was speaking retorted, *"Primo Uomo* Mossop. Your star has faded and now you do the bidding of a king of England who is even now trying to oppress the people of your own land, Ireland. There are other ways, Mr. Mossop, of making this land stable and prosperous."

Red faced, Henry Mossop snapped back, "This land can only survive if we import more slaves and obey the wishes of the King of England."

Another shouted, "Or of Spain, or France, or whoever pays you the most..."

Angered Henry Mossop proclaimed, "Should you follow this fool hearty plan of unifying to create a new governing body, you will fail. You will only succeed at the gracious hand of his majesty's indulgences."

"His indulgences!" Another shouted, "His capricious war-hungry greed, more like..."

"We need to provide for our own

families without the King as our distant parent!" …another scoffed.

Henry Mossop had to be restrained by his cohorts as he spat, "You are all doomed to an early grave! You had your chance to declare your loyalty to the King. But, instead, you demanded to hold this meeting. It is treasonous! You have been warned!"

The companions of Henry Mossop pushed him out the door and the room became eerily silent.

6 CHAPTER 75: (JUNE 1776) Eunice and TallMan At the Dunlap's Door

TallMan helped his mother, Eunice, up from the overstuffed down-filled cushions. He then rendered assistance to Polly, who was great with child. Mrs. Dunlap led the way, as the party wended its path toward the front door.

Simms, the Dunlap Butler, was already at the front door awaiting instructions.

"My other children are in Quebec,"

Eunice continued speaking with Mrs. Dunlap. "I came to the colonies for a final visit with my brother Stephen, and also to collect my son TallMan, then return home. I think at my age, I am quite done with travel and would prefer the comforts and routine of a loving family waiting for me in Canada."

TallMan mused, "During my search to learn how to heal, I have seen the hearts of men tear each other apart in battles. It saddens me that I cannot impose peace on these people before I leave."

"Peace?" Polly asked as she put both her hands on her lower back to try and ease the pressure of her unborn child.

"Some LongCoats profit from conflict, and have no interest in establishing peace with treaties," TallMan explained.

"No more fighting... No more battles... Is such a day even possible?" Mrs. Dunlap quipped. Polly replied, "To achieve peace, everyone must be at peace first, I think."

"I disagree..." TallMan started, "It will be a struggle to unite any force in a common goal of peace. It will be a fight to convince others that peace will benefit both sides. It will be a blood bath before peace can become a reality. And if, by a miracle, peace and unity are achieved in the land, then it will be a fading memory in future generations and they will forget the cost of peace and freedom."

"That philosophy seems rather odd for a doctor or medicine man to take. Are you promoting the shedding of men's blood? Is there not some Greek oath all men of medicine abide by to preserve life?" Polly mused.

"The Hippocratic Oath," TallMan explained, "demands medicine men heal and do no harm." He inhaled, "...but how can I heal a man if his civilization is more wounded than he? What of a civilization, which promotes harm to others? Needless violence, kidnappings, and enslavements?"

Polly asked, "I am curious, TallMan. Why are you concerned about the goings on of the colonies? Why is it important to you that we be at peace? Your home is far away..."

TallMan replied, "I will answer as a man of medicine. Disease spreads if left untreated. Your unrest, your battles will... your values will spread to my territory and will harm it. The disease was started in the palaces of kingdoms far away. It has spread to these shores. It has infected other tribes. Something must be done. Perhaps your people could develop a new profitable product instead of always fighting..."

Mrs. Dunlap added, "Oh, you mean we can make money in other ways besides selling well-bred ladies as slaves?" she glanced at Polly.

Eunice, feeling aches in her joints moved slowly as she said, "Slave raids are propelled by politics and greed."

Polly groaned recalling the time when her family lived in splendor. Then the King in England decided raiding the Irish villages for slaves served his purposes. Her family was torn apart.

Eunice continued, "A few profit from conflict. That means to continue the profit, they must manipulate colonists and tribes and any other peoples to encourage conflict." She looked at Polly, "It happened to you and your husband, Polly. It happened to me as a girl."

Polly responded with, "Is there nothing to be done? It seems hopeless. Is there no advice, nor path, to lead us out of this tempest."

Eunice smiled kindly, "The advice I can share is the same as that which my father gave me. Always pray to God for wisdom. Ask that He show you your personal path. One step each day. God really can turn the most horrific events into something good for His Children... sometimes in ways we cannot predict, Polly. *Romans 8:28*."

"You mean," Polly laughed abruptly in disbelief as she touched her skirts which concealed her unborn baby, "that now I barely escaped the clutches of the men who killed my husband and I will have my first child... alone... God can somehow make that... truly good?"

7 CHAPTER 76: (JUNE 1776) At Mrs. Dunlap's Front Door

The small party stood at the door in the foyer of the Dunlap home.

Simms, the Dunlap butler, stood motionless, silently listening to the conversation of TallMan, his mother Eunice, Polly, and of course, Mrs. Dunlap, mistress of that household.

TallMan looked at Polly, and offered, "One day, your child may make a difference in this world. A slight course correction which will change the lives of many for the good."

Polly shook her head, "Time will reveal my future slowly, I suppose... I must be patient."

Mrs. Dunlap added, "You won't be alone, Dear. I'll be with you. I know it is not the same as having your husband, but I am quite good with small humans, I assure you. Cling to hope. Force yourself to think enthusiastically about the future." Mrs. Dunlap splashed her brightest smile across her face, nodding.

Then Mrs. Dunlap added, "TallMan, I am sure your travels have not been placid. How do you remain hopeful?"

TallMan stated simply, "The sacrifice God made by sending His Son in my place to pay for my debts, my sins, encourages me to make a choice for good each day. One cannot be neutral and allow evil to fester around us, stepping over it as one does a muddy puddle. No,

I force myself to actively do good, even if I do not see the reward of my efforts immediately."

"Quite," Mrs. Dunlap nodded, "I understand how Christianity or Catholicism may instill a conscience into a group of savages... even ones who may have been bribed or threatened to do the bidding of some capricious wealthy entity. Of course, we all have a story about dealing with slave raiders, don't we?"

Polly looked at Mrs. Dunlap. "Mrs. Dunlap," Polly started, "You know my story, which brought me to fortunately be in your charge. You have heard Eunice's story... I have never asked you... do YOU have a story, Mrs. Dunlap?"

"Well," Mrs. Dunlap smiled shyly, "I am married to a newspaper man, so I know many stories..."

"I see," Eunice nodded.

"Of your personal experience?" Polly clarified.

"No," Mrs. Dunlap smiled, "Not first-hand experience, but a rather good story nonetheless. Oh! If you have a moment, 'tis quite fascinating... care to hear it?"

TallMan smiled, "Your enthusiasm, Mrs. Dunlap, piques my interest. I would very much like to hear the story."

"Excellent," Mrs. Dunlap looked at her butler Simms, "This may take an extra moment or two, Simms."

"I await your orders at your convenience, Madam Dunlap," Simms stated, secretly enjoying the banter. He was going to have much to share in the servant's hall tonight as the staff would dine after serving the Dunlap family their dinner.

"Oh, it is quite good," Mrs. Dunlap brightly said to Polly and TallMan.

8 CHAPTER 77: (JUNE 1776) Peter Timothy Leads Them To The Barn

Billy Dawes slowed the horses as his passenger, Peter Timothy, had thumped on the carriage roof to indicate Dawes should halt. Silversmith, who was sitting atop the carriage next to Billy Dawes, squinted her eyes and peered at the barn, doubtful.

She gave a puzzled look to Billy asking softly, "Is this barn? Really? The location where a secret meeting will take place with Benjamin Franklin?"

Billy replied to Silversmith, "Just because Peter Timothy is the son of the author Miss Jane told you to seek out..."

"I didn't know Peter's mother had died some time ago..." Silversmith interrupted, "Perhaps I should not trust people with two first names as their Christian and Surname."

"That matters not, Silversmith..." Billy explained, "Mr. Timothy is a new acquaintance we just met at the bookstore. Perhaps he simply doesn't know where the meeting will take place."

"You had best clarify matters with Mr. Timothy, then, Billy." Silversmith urged, "Miss Jane has entrusted us with this mission and I daresay we must succeed in finding how to contact Ambassador Benjamin Franklin so that Miss Jane can ask him to write an official letter requesting cessation of slave raids."

"Right," Billy affirmed, "So innocents like Miss Polly Mulhoolin don't end up on the side of the road having just escaped from an Indian raid."

"And," Silversmith reminded, "to give Miss Jane peace that she fulfilled whatever her uncle Floyd was working on before he died. Only then, can she move forward."

Nodding in agreement, Billy Dawes, carriage driver, twisted around to speak down to the carriage below. Mr. Peter Timothy remained inside.

Billy Dawes tried to be discrete and asked, "A barn, Sir? Is this barn the location of the secret meeting with Mr. Franklin?"

Peter Timothy leaned out the carriage door window to answer Billy Dawes, "Remember when I told you that Susanna Wright and Ben Franklin meet?" Peter started, "I have heard Susanna Wright is one of the scouts to find locations so as to not be interrupted by the King's men. I heard that this barn is the newest location selected by Miss Wright. Inside, we should find several like-minded souls discussing matters of this land and discussing what can and cannot be changed."

"Discussing, sir?" Silversmith asked.

Peter Timothy replied, "I believe it is something political, but other than that, I am unaware of the nature of their meetings or how many are in attendance... in that unassuming barn."

Silversmith shrugged her shoulders at Billy Dawes and softly commented, "I suppose we could investigate."

"If we walk into that barn, they will know we are outsiders and I fear a hostile reaction, Silversmith." Billy warned.

"Oh, look," Peter Timothy remarked leaning out the window as he saw the barn door open, "You can see along the hill over there the stable boys must be exercising the horses... and there is a fellow dressed in finery. Oh and there are others with him? Do you two see them in the distance? Over there, exiting from the barn. His presence is proof enough there was a meeting of some sort in there." Peter continued, observing, triumphantly, "And, you can see the doors closing behind him, so there must be others still inside."

Billy Dawes, prepared carriage driver, reached into his leather bag behind him and extracted a spyglass to get a better look at the view some distance away.

"I don't recognize any of those men," Billy shared as he handed the spyglass to Silversmith.

Silversmith extended the unit and peered with one eye at the barn. "I recognize him! That's the Opera Singer. That *primo uomo*. Henry Mossop sang at the Wilson Estate. Miss Jane met him! What is he doing here? I think that's proof enough that this may be the right place."

Satisfied, Silversmith slid off the carriage to the ground.

After her feet softly hit the ground, Silversmith leaned into the carriage. "Thank you so much, Mr. Timothy, for showing us this place. I am so sorry I never got a chance to have met your mother, but I look forward to reading her book. The one Mr. Dawes purchased."

Before Peter Timothy nor Billy Dawes could stop Silversmith, she scampered silently away toward the barn. In a harsh whisper, Billy exclaimed, "Silversmith! Stop! We don't know what danger lurks there!"

Silversmith, hearing Billy's concern, walked back two strides to the carriage and responded in as loud a whisper as she could while she looked up to Billy, still sitting on his perch atop the carriage. Silversmith hoarsely replied, "To hear what they are saying... I must get closer."

"But, I've got the horses..." Billy protested. " We could ride over there."

"I do not believe," Silversmith countered, "that those men would speak freely if a horse drawn carriage were to charge up to them. Nay, they may even cease speaking altogether. I must make haste before they finish their conversation."

"But..." Billy Dawes spoke uneasily.

"Could you, Billy..." Silversmith interrupted him, "Please remain here with Mr. Timothy and your loud horses, so that I may creep closer to hear them? You may watch over me with your spyglass. I will remain in the shadows... I will be subtle..."

Silversmith smiled and tip toed toward the barn before waiting for Billy Dawes to respond.

Silversmith stepped through the line of corn stalks in a narrow patch of corn fields lining the road. The clearing around the barn was dotted with eight foot tall hay stacks, plenty of cover for her to hide behind as she listened to the conversation of Henry Mossop, the opera singer who had performed at the estate of Lady Sarah Wilson.

Silversmith gathered her skirt hem up, so she could move more quickly.

Nervous, Billy Dawes extended his spyglass to watch Silversmith hide behind one huge haystacks and then quickly dash to the next haystack, wending her way closer to the men engrossed in conversation just outside the barn entrance.

Peter Timothy eased himself out of the carriage and climbed up to sit on the perch near the Billy Dawes, where there was a better vantage point to observe.

Peter whispered to Billy, "How is she faring?"

"She's just gotten close enough, I think, to overhear, because she is remaining quite still at one hay stack in particular," Billy reported, as he peered through his spyglass.

9 CHAPTER 78: (June 1776) 1697
Story of Hannah

Still in the foyer of the Dunlap residence, Mrs. Dunlap was pleased her small audience wanted to hear her story even if it was not one which had happened to Mrs. Dunlap personally. Mrs. Dunlap often boasted about being married to John Dunlap, the printer, and how she could read things perhaps most others would not have access to. She enjoyed being able to share stories at tea time. Mrs. Dunlap rubbed her hands together in anticipation as she, Polly, TallMan and his mother Eunice, awaited her story. Simms, her butler stood stoically near the front door.

Mrs. Dunlap turned to Eunice and started with, "Well, about a hundred years before your story, Eunice... You realize, this is a true story... oh, it is quite good, indeed! Yes... where to begin... Well, let me set the scene."

"Please do," Eunice urged.

Mrs. Dunlap stepped back as if she were on an imaginary stage. She began to elaborate with animated hands. "Picture half a dozen homes in the wilderness of Massachusetts about a century ago... late 1690's... There Hannah Duston, a Puritan mother of nine children, was taken captive. Oh, not alone, mind you, as your husband was taken alone Polly. Nay, Hannah was abducted with her aunt and her midwife, Mary Neff. Oh! And about forty neighbors all from Massachusetts. I think it was by the Abenaki... Oh! No offense to you Eunice and TallMan... of course, we are all friends here."

"Quite," Eunice replied.

Mrs. Dunlap continued, "Well, details are not important. Anyway it was some time during King William's war... I think. I'll have to ask John... Oh, I mean Mr. Dunlap, when he returns from the printing presses."

Polly interjected, "So, abducting colonists to be slaves has been going on for a very long time..."

"Polly, you've already shared your story!" Mrs. Dunlap protested, somewhat dismayed the group's attention had suddenly been taken away from her.

"My apologies for interrupting, Mrs. Dunlap." Polly smiled, "Please continue."

Happy once more, Mrs. Dunlap cleared her throat and squinted her eyes as if peering into the past, "Imagine a cold snowy winter. Imagine being yanked from your bed one gray morning only to see your wood and brick house burned to the ground. Imagine you have just had a child and your one-week old infant starts to cry. You are helpless. You witness one of your Indian attackers pick up your babe and strike it against a tree until silenced. Imagine..."

Then Mrs. Dunlap gasped and changed her tone evaluating Polly's reaction.

Mrs. Dunlap said, "Oh, Polly, it's not predictive of your situation. You haven't even had your babe, yet."

"Nonetheless," Polly replied flinching, , "Not a comforting image you have asked me to imagine."

"Yes...well... Your story and Eunice's story had elements of dismay, so I felt it appropriate I should do likewise..." Mrs. Dunlap defended.

"Please do continue," Eunice urged, "This all happened before TallMan was even born, so we do not take it personally, do we, TallMan?" She looked up at her son.

TallMan replied, "Abenaki and Colonist alike can make wise and poor choices. I take no offense."

"And what," Polly asked, "...of Hanna's husband and all her other children?"

"Oh," Mrs. Dunlap frowned, trying to recall, "I think her husband was in the field."

"So, he escaped?" Polly asked hopefully.

"Well," Mrs. Dunlap tapped her lip as she thought, "The Indians were given guns and ammunition by some of the wealthy merchants in the colonies. Could have been the same merchants from which Hannah's family bought their firearms."

"So," Polly stopped the story, "Those

who sell weapons, armed both sides with the same weapons?"

"As I said," TallMan explained, "They can only profit if there is conflict. Many don't believe it, but this story simply confirms my suspicious that selling ammunition supplies and selling slaves has been so lucrative for so long to those in power."

Eunice added, "It encourages merchants to pledge their allegiance to profits and not to their country. It encourages merchants to abandon moral decency and blur the lines of right and wrong."

"May I continue?" Mrs. Dunlap asked, "I want to finish..."

"Please," Eunice encouraged, "We understand you are recollecting this story from memory and we do not expect you to reiterate every detail with accuracy."

Mrs. Dunlap adopted a very pious

expression as she continued, "I shall try my best to keep the attentions of you, my audience," Mrs. Dunlap cleared her throat. "Let me see. Ah, yes, when Hannah's husband, Thomas, discovered the attack, he mounted his steed and raced to his house to warn his older children, who were playing outside. Thomas did get his children to safety."

"That is most encouraging," Polly sighed.

Mrs. Dunlap shot Polly a look and continued, "But, weakened by recent birth, stoically Puritan mother Hannah was left inside the house, defenseless. Oh, and her aunt, who was acting as her midwife, Mary Neff, was there, as well. Anyway, those raiding the village rounded up the slow slow-moving prey, such as Hannah Duston and her aunt Mary Neff."

"So, only her young baby died?" Eunice asked, reliving her own raid as a girl.

"Well," Mrs. Dunlap explained

hesitantly, "In that group of homes, twenty seven were killed, and thirteen taken captive. They were raiding small villages, you see... to round up slaves... not future daughters, as became, Eunice."

"What happened next?" TallMan asked.

Delighted her audience seemed attentive, Mrs. Dunlap continued, "The Abenaki Indians who raided the clearing forced their captives to walk a hundred miles into the wilderness. Now in calf-deep snow, you can only march about a dozen miles a day. Those who could not keep up on the 15-day journey were Toma-hawked." Mrs. Dunlap looked at TallMan, "Is that how you say it?" She imitated the motion of using a small ax on some victim.

"I believe we all can understand your meaning, Mrs. Dunlap," TallMan replied.

"Good. Good," Mrs. Dunlap muttered to herself before continuing, "Their reward for surviving that snowy journey was that they could live to become a slave. Along the way, I heard that some colonist captives were taught Indian songs to entertain their captors when they rested for the night. Fifteen nights in the snow... can you imagine? Unlike the tribe which adopted Eunice, only one of Hannah's captors had converted to Christianity."

"Only one?" Eunice asked.

Mrs. Dunlap looked at Eunice and replied, "Yes, and that fellow converted, I believe, when he was sent to capture Mary Rolandson, a reverend's wife. He called Christianity 'The English Way', whereas he said the bloodthirsty wars promoted by the French was the 'French Way'."

Polly asked, "Did your leading lady, Hannah ever talk to this converted Indian captor?"

10 CHAPTER 79: (June 1776) 1697
The English Way vs. The French Way

The small group stood in the foyer of Mrs. Dunlap's home intently listening to Mrs. Dunlap's story of Hannah, the Puritan mother of nine children, who had witnessed her newborn babe being killed by one of her captors. Mrs. Dunlap had assured them all that Hannah's story ended differently than Polly's or Eunice's story. They all listened intently.

Mrs. Dunlap replied, "I believe that Christian Indian fellow told Hannah, if God would open the path to deliver her from captivity, it shall be so. However, he did share that his companions encouraged him to leave the English Way and go back to the more profitable French Way. It was a struggle for him."

Polly mused, "I wonder what Hannah was thinking at that moment. Was her Puritan faith strengthened or weakened when one of her captors shared that God might deliver her from captivity and a future of slavery. I mean, was he implying if she escaped, he would not stop her?"

Eunice added, "I was not aware that slave raids on Colonial residents was going on for so long. I assumed my situation was unique."

Polly added, "Before our cabin was attacked, I heard gossip in town about King George funding such raids to teach pioneers, such as myself, a lesson. That we cannot live without a monarch's indulgence. I assumed it was a desire of the British empire... yet, Hannah's story indicates her raid was perhaps directed by the French monarchy."

"When these monarchs are uncertain," TallMan interjected, "about their capability to rule, they resort to harsh tactics to try and suppress a more powerful ruler from displacing them."

"Exactly, TallMan!" Mrs. Dunlap smiled, triumphantly, "My story of Hannah demonstrates that whoever is in power, undoubtedly has the money to hire native tribes to capture and enslave colonists who disagree with their pecuniary policies."

Eunice added, "And it seems they will do this until somebody stops them..."

Polly challenged, "So, who then is to blame? The visible tribes who do the actual raids or the invisible wealthy men who hire them?"

Polly looked down to think and then took a breath and asked, "And was Hannah Duston sold as an expensive European born slave? Was she herded onto a ship to be sold in a foreign land? Did she end up being adopted into a family, as Eunice had?"

"Well," Mrs. Dunlap inhaled slowly, "the ending of Hannah's story is a bit different than yours, Polly or yours, Eunice..."

"Oh! She died?" Polly asked in dismay.

Mrs. Dunlap shook her head no and answered Polly with, "Hannah, and her aunt, Mary, befriended a young European fellow captive. He was but a youth of a boy named Samuel. He had been captured a year earlier. Another Indian... oh, I think his name was Bampico..."

"The names matter not, Mrs. Dunlap. Please go on," Polly urged.

"Yes, yes, Dear," Mrs. Dunlap continued, "So, this Indian youth named *Bampico* taught European Samuel to strike a man in the temple and use the tomahawk to kill quickly. Samuel quietly shared this knowledge with Hannah, at her request."

"Why would she want to learn that?" Polly asked.

TallMan and Eunice looked at each other, then back at Mrs. Dunlap.

Mrs. Dunlap continued, "Well, on the fifteenth day of her capture, Hannah killed nine of her captors and spared one Indian boy, who escaped with a squaw."

"Was it," Polly asked, "The boy who had learned the Christian English Way and wanted to leave the violent French Way?"

"That I do not know for certain, Dear..." Mrs. Dunlap replied, "Could have been. Later, it was reported that two injured Indians staggered into

93

another camp bearing seven wounds. Samuel, merely a boy himself, killed one of his captors. Ten dead total."

"It was as if your Hannah," TallMan started, "Was trying to avenge the deaths of her newborn babe and her dozen or so neighbors... life for a life..."

"Or," Eunice suggested, "Just that she needed to eliminate the entire party of captors before she could completely escape. If she had waited until she was sold or traded as a slave, I doubt she could have planned such an attack and lived."

"You mean the captives killed all their original captors?" Polly asked Mrs. Dunlap.

"Oh, yes. Hannah led the escape. She donned the clothing of those she slew. She took a canoe and scuttled the other canoes to avoid being followed. She also filled up the canoe with all the firearms the French had supplied to their Indian hirelings."

"So, Hannah, her aunt, Mary and this boy Samuel escaped?" Polly asked.

Mrs. Dunlap replied, "I told you, Hannah's ending was a bit different than either of yours."

"How long did it take Hannah and the others to row to safety?" Polly asked.

"Wait. The tale continues..." Mrs. Dunlap whispered, "Once in the canoe, she had forgotten something, and rowed back again to shore."

"What? And risk other Indians coming in response to the cries of attack? What could she have forgotten that was so important?" Polly inquired.

Awkwardly, Mrs. Dunlap squirmed a bit and said, "Understand, I'm merely reporting the story as I recall it. I mean no offense to Eunice nor to you, TallMan. It is just a story from a long, long time ago."

"I take no offense, Mrs. Dunlap. Please go on," TallMan urged.

Mrs. Dunlap paused a moment, took a deep breath and crossed her arms, then continued, "Hannah left her aunt Mary and young Samuel in the canoe. Then, she marched back to her fresh slaughter and there scalped all ten of the dead. She wrapped the scalps in one of the tapestries stolen from her home during the raid. Then, she returned to the canoe with her grisly baggage and they headed again to Boston."

"Why would she scalp the Indians?" Polly asked horrified and confused. "It is as if she became like the people she hated. She had been prey, and now became the hunter..."

Mrs. Dunlap explained, "The General Court in Boston actually paid Hanna twenty-five pounds for her scalps and another twenty-five went to Samuel and Mary to share."

"I am amazed you have recalled so

many details from this century old tale, Mrs. Dunlap..." Eunice marveled, "You told it with vivid imagery."

"Well, Eunice, before Hannah was reunited with her husband and remaining children... and before she gave birth to another daughter, Lydia in 1698, Hannah was invited to visit a couple of prominent fellows, who had her story documented. I actually read it again after I met you, awaiting the right moment to tell it!" Mrs. Dunlap clapped her hands together, pleased.

"Well told, Mrs. Dunlap. With whom did Hannah visit?" Eunice asked.

Delighted to continue the story, although it was not hers, Mrs. Dunlap offered, "A judge, who was also a printer, and a hater of the slave trade, Samuel Sewall. He wrote 'The Selling of Joseph', you know. Joseph from the Bible? The one sold into slavery by his brothers? Not the blessed Mary's husband."

"This Samuel Sewall, I have not heard of him," TallMan started, "What was his philosophy?"

Mrs. Dunlap smiled brightly as she continued, " 'The Selling of Joseph', I think, was Mr. Sewall's way of saying that even the Bible is against slavery. I suspect his little work was the first anti-slave publication in all the colonies. You see, TallMan, Mr. Sewall believed that a man's station should be decided by his own choices in life. Mr. Sewall felt the frenzied greed, which fuels a slave raid, not only disrupts the lives of innocents, and deprives society of a positive contributor, but also robs each man of his right to choose his own path in life..." Mrs. Dunlap explained.

Eunice spoke up, "So stealing a man, not only robs the colonial village of a worker, but deprives society of a person who can leave a legacy... thus the injury is not merely to the individual, but to the whole tribe, village or nation..."

Mrs. Dunlap continued, "And Hannah met the man who penned her story. The one I read. Preacher, Mr. Cotton Mather, who wrote about it in his *Magnalia Christi Americana*. Mr. Mather drew an analogy between Hanna Duston and Jael in the Bible. You know, the one who gave milk to Sisera and then stabbed him in the head with a tent peg, killing him?"

Mrs. Dunlop's audience gasped.

Mrs. Dunlop smiled, pleased, and went on to boast, "Being married to a printer permits me the luxury of reading... well, printed material, which creates interesting conversations over tea."

"When will people learn," TallMan commented, "that society gains strength from collaboration, fair consistent rules, encouragement of learning and honing the talents of one another? Slavery breeds contempt, rebellion, and murderous intentions."

"Well," Mrs. Dunlap announced triumphantly, "Hasn't this been cozy that we all could share share a story about an Indian slave raid? And now, I assume you both wish to get to your hired carriage and head to Canada."

Eunice replied, "Actually, we are on our way to *Kanata*. That was the original Iroquois word. It means 'village settlement'. I do hope we can all remain friends and somehow communicate..."

"Yes, is that possible?" Polly asked, "I would very much like to remain friends with you both," she said to TallMan and his mother, Eunice.

Mrs. Dunlap signaled Simms, the butler, with a glance.

Simms opened the door, but on the other side was a messenger about to knock.

The messenger froze startled to see so many people looking at him. He was panting for breath as he had just run a long distance.

"A matter of some urgency, Sir." The messenger boy handed a paper to Simms, the butler, who reached into his pocket and gave the boy a coin.

The boy nodded curtly and ran off to his next assignment.

11 CHAPTER 80: (JUNE 1776) Fuming By The Haystack

The small group of men, led by fading opera *Primo Uomo* Henry Mossop, stood out in the shadows of the fading sun as rays changed from yellow to red and slipped below the outline of the barn, casting long shadows on the eight foot tall haystacks.

Henry Mossop fumed, "I have never been so insulted as a man of business, nor have I been so insulted as a performer." Henry stomped about waving his pudgy arms in the air, dismayed.

A breeze outside the barn was cool as he and his cohorts recalled the events which had just propelled Mr. Mossop firmly forth from the barn meeting.

"I am neither *primo* nor *secondo uomo* in small productions," Henry Mossop hissed, "But I am a primo man of business and none of those attendees shall be spared!"

His men countered, "but some praised you at Lady Sarah Wilson's estate."

"I mean," Henry tossed back, "The reviews of me in this wretched wilderness don't matter. I know my stage reviews have gotten worse and worse. That is why I became a man of business instead of a man of music."

"What think you, Mr. Mossop, of those men inside the barn and what they were saying?" another asked.

The tarnished opera singer snapped, "Those imbeciles! I cannot give credence to fools! The men and women inside that barn are all fools! I warned them, and now I shall inform his majesty." Mr. Mossop was perturbed once again for having to explain his point of view.

The men did not realize Silversmith was hovering mere feet away, hiding behind the façade of a haystack.

Another man asked, "Would any of those inside the barn, there, um... would any of them be able to damage our business plans?"

"That disorganized emotional tangled mess in the barn?" The opera singer sneered, "They could never get unified long enough to even write a letter to the king! No, they shall not change my plans for profit."

"We did what you asked. We held up our end of the agreement." Another man interjected, "You promised you'd pay off our debts of passage over here if we helped you," the man reminded Mossop.

"Not until," the opera singer slowly hissed, "I get my cargo aboard that ship and it sets sail! What punishment the king chooses to inflict on you is up to his soldiers here. If you want my protection, you need to prove to me that you are willing to take your neighbor and sell him to save your own hide."

Silversmith wished she could see him, but when she peeked around the haystack, the two men had their backs to her. Only the third, the opera singer, Henry Mossop, was facing her direction, but she already had recognized him. Luckily, Mr. Mossop was looking away from the haystack, which camouflaged Silversmith's location.

The opera singer reprimanded his men, "I paid you, to hire the tribes and collect white slaves for trade. You know I can get more money for selling an already skilled European who can speak more than one language. But you lost my cargo? Is that right? How! The Indians you hired actually allowed some to escape? The lazy lot! Reliable help is so difficult to find. You need to take pride in your work!"

"We have competition..." one man protested.

"Competition?" Henry Mossop's voice trembled in restrained sarcasm, "Competition? From whom? Those fellows who insist on importing slaves found in the mystic lands of Africa?"

"Well," another man said, "They ship far more in number so when some die or go missing during passage, they still have plenty to sell for profit," the fellow countered.

In frustration, opera singer Mossop fumed, "None of their cargo will sell at all if there isn't a customer willing to pay. We have a niche in that we provide slaves which already speak English, French, or German and they generally already know trade. This is a land aplenty. You should have no problem taking the numbers of white slaves we need for our inventory."

"But," the first man protested, "some don't like our hired Indians also taking the families and neighbors of the local colonists. They keep trying to find where we've hidden the captives. It's very inconvenient because sometimes they locate them and steal them back!"

"And that is," Henry Mossop, the opera singer explained, "precisely why I hired a local to take care of Floyd Hargreaves. He won't be assisting families in locating their abducted loved ones anymore. Hmm?"

"So our profits will be fatter when we ship this lot for sale?"

"Yes," Henry Mossop replied, "Once we ship them across the ocean so nobody can find them and allow them to escape."

"Therefore, we will take the opposite route of those who trade in black slaves?" the man asked.

Henry Mossop adopted the tone of a school instructor, "Why do you think they make the effort to collect cargo in Africa and ship it here? Because this land is foreign and there is not a soul here can help the black slave find a route home. Likewise, we must gather-up our local European Colonists who thought they had escaped the Monarch's whip. Then we ship and sell them in a land so far across the ocean, so foreign, so remote these colonists can only give up and accept the inescapable reality of their permanent slavery."

"With Floyd Hargreaves eliminated, will that niece of his be a problem?" Another man asked. Silversmith's mouth went dry.

She remained motionless.

The wind picked up bits of broken hay, which hit her face, causing her to squint.

Henry Mossop replied, "Our Patroness Lady Sarah Wilson has agreed to keep that annoying niece of Hargreaves at the estate until after we set sail. So Jane Hargreaves will not be an obstruction to our profits."

"I wouldn't want Jane Hargreaves to be harmed," one of the men said in such a soft voice Silversmith was barely able to discern the words in his sentence.

"Everything is evaluated," Henry Mossop reiterated, "as a cost of conducting business. How would I be able to afford the fine imported fabrics of the famous Tweedbottom tailor shop if I did not supplement my purse by doing the bidding of the Crown...."

The opera singer flipped up his coat collar and pulled his garment closer around his dough-like body as a shield from the evening breezes.

"Or Crowns," laughed the other man.

"Exactly. We work for whichever king will pay the most," Henry Mossop affirmed. "If all men were equal as those fools in that barn claim, then I would not be doing the bidding of a monarch, now would I? Today it is expedient for me to serve him. Others serve me... it is the way things are. We are all born to our positions."

Silversmith took a breath, in hopes of stifling a sneeze from the bits of hay floating around her face and in a deliberate move, she leaned over to see if she could catch a glimpse of the man indebted to the opera singer.

To her surprise, Silversmith did recognize one of the faces in the bright light of the moon. She gasped in shock. Quickly, she retreated back behind the hay stack.

That same man froze and lowered his voice. Speaking deliberately, he slowly turned his head in the direction of Silversmith's hay stack and ask the others, "Did you just hear something?"

12 What Just Happened?

Eunice shares her story, as does Mrs. Dunlap. It turns out, however, it was not Mrs. Dunlap's story, at all, but it was a story about Hannah, which took place a century earlier in 1697. Eunice explains her unusual adoption, and how she made peace with a life foisted upon her.

Silversmith and Billy have made headway, and Peter Timothy opens doors for their cause.

Meanwhile, the secret meeting revealed more than expected, especially from Button's perspective. Who would rule this land? The British or the French?

13 Did You Know...

The printer and publisher Mary Katherine Goddard (1738-1816) was entrusted with the task to make a true copy of the *Declaration of Independence* in 1777. Her copy contained the printed names of all the signers, but John Hancock took quill and ink and signed her copy as proof that Mary Goddard's replica was an accurate typeset version of the original *Declaration of Independence*, which had inked handwritten signatures of all the Founding Fathers.

Goddard's brother, William, and her widowed mother, worked with Mary to set up a weekly newspaper in Providence,

Rhode Island called the *Providence Gazette.*

In 1768, she followed her brother, who was in Philadelphia, where he published one of the Colonies' largest newspapers, the *Pennsylvania Chronicle.* She managed the daily functions of the *Pennsylvania Chronicle* newspaper.

In 1773, her brother established the first Baltimore newspaper, the *Maryland Journal.* When the *Pennsylvania Chronicle* closed down, Mary Goddard moved to Baltimore so that she could manage the *Maryland Journal.*

Starting on May 10, 1775, a year after Mary Goddard had joined the impartial unbiased paper, it carried the colophon "Published by M. K. Goddard".

The **colophon** was an emblem or statement used by printers to indicate who authored the work and other printing details. Typically it could be found on the spine, end, or cover of most printed works.

Also in 1775, Mary Katherine Goddard became the postmaster of Baltimore, and it is very likely she was the first woman appointed to such a position in the Colonies.

Her ethical and unbiased integrity gained her the respect of hundreds of business men, including Ebenezer Hazard and Thomas Jefferson.

On January 18, 1777, the American Second Continental Congress moved that a true copy of the *Declaration of Independence* be widely distributed to the public. Goddard offered the use of her printing press.

Because of her sterling reputation, it is thought that this is why Mary Goddard was one of the few selected for the important task of issuing a formal copy of the *Declaration of Independence* to be distributed throughout the Colonies.

She bravely printed her full name on every copy as it was distributed during the American Revolution (1775-1783) against the English king.

This was at a time when the British monarch had declared that any person who put their name to anything which opposed the crown could be accused of treason. King George II enforced an archaic law nicknamed the "Bloody Code", which lasted from 1688 to 1815. In the code were listed 50 offenses punishable by death. In 1765, the number of offenses rose to 160 and by 1815 the offenses demanding the death penalty grew to 225.

This "Bloody Code" justified supervised torture with the support of the King. Types of sanctioned torture included water-boarding, stretching machines, whipping post, stocks, branding, drawing and quartering (using horses to pull a person apart), burning at the stake, and more.

So, imagine the risks Mary Goddard took simply by publicly putting her name in print on distributed copies of the *Declaration of Independence*, as well as in the colophon of her newspaper. Her acts demonstrated bravery and courage on behalf of liberty.

Information compiled from various sources including Maryland State Archives and University of Michigan.

1777 copy of the United States Declaration of Independence - Library of Congress, Rare Books and Special Collections Division, Continental Congress & Constitutional Convention, Broadside Collection.

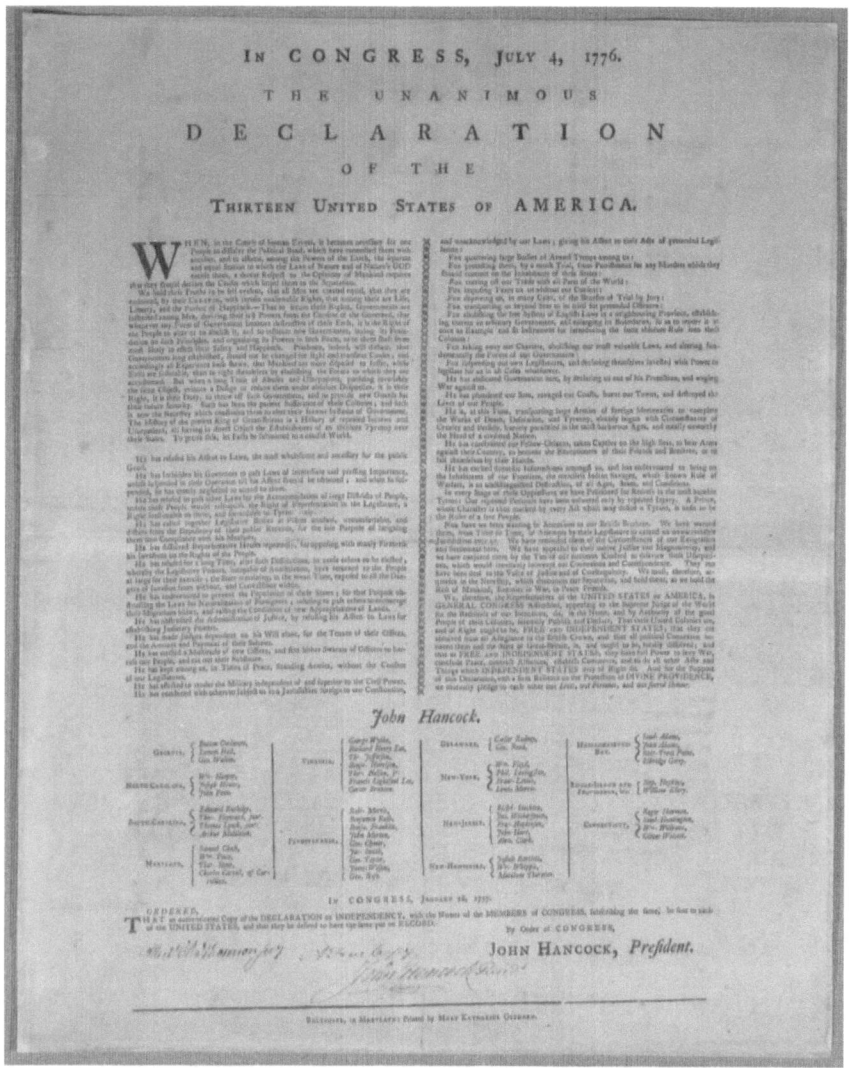

1777 copy of the United States Declaration of Independence - Library of Congress, Rare Books and Special Collections Division, Continental Congress & Constitutional Convention, Broadside Collection.

14 Vocabulary

In the early 1770s, before the colonies united into the United States of America, some words and terms were used, which may be explained in this section.

Acquaintance: A person known to you, but not a close friend.

Consternation: Extreme surprise with confusion and fear.

Colophon: An emblem or statement used by printers to indicate who authored the work and other printing details. Typically it could be found on the spine, end, or cover of most printed works.

Primo Uomo This is an Italian term for the words "First Man". Often in opera, a female star is called the *Prima Donna*, or the First Lady. The back up would be *Seconda Donna* or the backup man would be *Secondo Uomo*. These are terms to reference status on the stage.

Reciprocate: To share the same feelings. When someone gives you a gift, you give a gift in return.

Statuesque: Tall and beautiful.

ABOUT THE AUTHOR

Wynter Sommers is the pseudonym for an American writing team. The team consists of technology specialists, PhD's, and other field-tested experts.

With over thirty years of in-classroom experience, the authors artistically weave subtle meaning into each narrative to lend lasting appeal to this new classic, which encourage repeated readings.

By reading an enjoyable fictional adventure, the reader learns many educational topics and hones their skills in US History, civics, vocabulary and reading comprehension, critical thinking, social studies and more.

Each time a story theme is explored, new meaning is revealed. Objective facts in the "Did you know" section stimulate conversation, provoking heartfelt introspection on various topics. Daily actions of everyday characters placed in extraordinary situations, demonstrate the consequences of their choices. These are the same choices you and I may need to make. These stories highlight the value of choosing peace, honor, integrity, truth, patience and perseverance to overcome obstacles in real life. Wynter Sommers hopes each tale inspires action, creativity, and kindness towards your neighbor. One never knows when a small choice today will impacted generations into the future. Choose wisely. True love is the toughest substance on earth.

Wynter Sommers hopes you will enjoy the other BJORN ESTERDAY WAS NOT BORN YESTERDAY stories in this series.